JUDGE DREDD

JUSTICE ONE

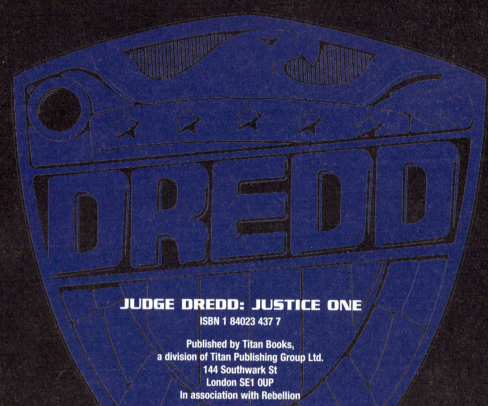

JUDGE DREDD: JUSTICE ONE

ISBN 1 84023 437 7

Published by Titan Books,
a division of Titan Publishing Group Ltd.
144 Southwark St
London SE1 0UP
In association with Rebellion

A CIP catalogue record for this title is available from the British Library.

First edition: April 2002
1 3 5 7 9 10 8 6 4 2

Cover illustration by John Higgins.

Printed in Italy.

Other *2000 AD* titles now available from Titan Books:

Judge Dredd: Emerald Isle (ISBN: 1 84023 341 9)
Judge Dredd: Death Aid (ISBN: 1 84023 344 3)
Judge Dredd featuring Judge Death (ISBN: 1 84023 386 9)
Judge Dredd: Goodnight Kiss (ISBN: 1 84023 346 X)
Judge Dredd: Helter Skelter (ISBN: 1 84023 348 6)

The Complete Ballad of Halo Jones (ISBN: 1 84023 342 7)
The Complete D.R. & Quinch (ISBN: 1 84023 345 1)
A.B.C. Warriors: The Mek-Nificent Seven (ISBN: 1 84023 347 8)
Sláine The King (ISBN: 1 84023 416 4)

To order from the UK telephone 01536 764 646

What did you think of this book? We love to hear from our readers. Please email us at: readerfeedback@titanemail.com, or write to us at the above address.

JUSTICE ONE

Featuring TALKBACK,
A MAN CALLED GREENER,
TWILIGHT'S LAST GLEAMING
and EX-MEN

Garth Ennis ● John Burns
Peter Doherty ● Glenn Fabry
John Higgins ● Anthony Williams

TITAN BOOKS
in association with *2000 AD*

"JUSTICE ONE"

(originally published in *2000 AD* Progs #766–771)
Writer — Garth Ennis
Artist — Peter Doherty
Letterer — Tom Frame

"TALKBACK"

(originally published in *2000 AD* Prog #740)
Writer — Garth Ennis
Artist — Glenn Fabry
Letterer — Tom Frame

"A MAN CALLED GREENER"

(originally published in *2000 AD* Prog #828)
Writer — Garth Ennis
Artist — Anthony Williams
Letterer — Tom Frame

"TWILIGHT'S LAST GLEAMING"

(originally published in *2000 AD* Progs #754–756)
Writer — Garth Ennis
Artist — John Burns
Letterer — Tom Frame

"EX-MEN"

(originally published in *2000 AD* Prog #818)
Writer — Garth Ennis
Artist — John Higgins
Letterer — Tom Frame

Garth Ennis

Garth Ennis burst onto the comics scene in 1988, with the controversial *Troubled Souls* (originally published in UK magazine *Crisis*). Taking over from long-time *Judge Dredd* scribe, John Wagner, Ennis wrote well over 100 gripping, bloody episodes centring on life and law in Mega-City One. He was then recruited by DC Comics, for whom he wrote *Hellblazer*, with artist Steve Dillon, and *Goddess*. Then came *Preacher*, Ennis and Dillon's multi award-winning magnum opus. Currently, Ennis is writing *Punisher*, *Fury*, and *War Story*, a series of hard-hitting Second World War one-shots.

John Burns

John Burns is a prolific *2000 AD* artist, having illustrated series as diverse as *Judge Dredd*, *Black Light*, and *Vector 13*. He is also a long-running illustrator of Robbie Morrison's *Nikolai Dante*. Outside of the Galaxy's Greatest Comic, his work includes *Espers* and the *James Bond* tale, 'A Silent Armageddon'.

Peter Doherty

Peter Doherty has worked exclusively on *Dredd*–related material for *2000 AD*, with 'Justice One' representing his longest individual run on the Judge, although he also drew the *Judge Death* miniseries 'Boyhood of a Superfiend' and contributed to the epic 'Judgement Day'. His US work includes *Grendel Tales*.

Glenn Fabry

Glenn Fabry is now internationally renowned for an unbroken run of cover paintings spanning 66 issues of *Preacher* and associated one-shots. His *2000 AD* resumé includes occasional material for *Judge Dredd*, but his most influential work is his run on *Sláine*. Glenn's work has graced the covers of Garth Ennis' *Adventures in the Rifle Brigade* series for DC comics, and Jamie Delano's *Outlaw Nation*.

John Higgins

John Higgins has an extensive *2000 AD* history, including artwork for *Chopper*, *Freaks*, and collaborations with both Alan Moore and Peter Milligan on '*Future Shocks*'. His bibliography also features colouring for Moore's classic *Watchmen*, work on *Mutatis*, the Jamie Delano-scripted *World Without End*, Garth Ennis' *Pride and Joy*, and his own *Razorjack*.

Anthony Williams

Anthony Williams began his comics career at Marvel UK, at which time he drew everything from *The Real Ghostbusters* to *Action Force* and *Transformers*. Over at DC Comics, his credits include *Justice League*, *The Flash* and *Resurrection Man*, while at Marvel (US) he drew *Captain America*, *X-Men* and *Punisher*. For *2000 AD*, Williams has drawn *Kola Commandos*, *Robo-Hunter* and *Mean Arena*.

THE GALAXY'S GREATEST COMIC...

Published in the UK on 26 February 1977, Prog 1 of *2000 AD* ushered in a new era of sci-fi action and adventure for comic readers, dazzling them with a mind-blowing array of fantastic futures and shocking possibilities. Appearing for the first time in Prog 2, *Judge Dredd* made a huge and instant impression with readers and remains the mainstay of *2000 AD* to this day. In the twenty-five years and 1280 (and counting) progs that followed, *2000 AD* has continued to thrill and inspire legions of fans, with memorable strips such as *A.B.C Warriors*, *D.R. & Quinch*, *The Ballad of Halo Jones*, *Nemesis the Warlock*, *Robo-Hunter*, *Strontium Dog* and *Zenith* (to mention but a few).

2000 AD was the proving ground for a host of A-list British writers and artists, now recognised both sides of the Atlantic. Luminaries to emerge from under the wing of Tharg The Mighty (*2000 AD*'s alien editor for the uninitiated) include Brian Bolland, Garth Ennis, Alan Grant, Alan Moore, Grant Morrison, Frank Quitely and many, many more.

Titan Books' links with *2000 AD* go back almost to the very beginning, with the publication of the first graphic novel collection, *The Chronicles of Judge Dredd*, back in July 1981.

Mega-Speak

2000 AD introduced fans not only to new worlds and new characters, but also to a whole new language. From the alien utterings of Tharg ("Zarjaz", which means great, "Thrill-power", which quantified the amount of excitement in a given strip, and "Borag Thungg", a greeting, became common parlance among fans of the comic) to the street lingo of Mega-City One, *2000 AD* quickly developed its very own dictionary. For those unfamiliar with the world of Judge Dredd, here's a handy guide to Mega-speak:

PSI-JUDGE

BLOCK WAR: Conflict between rival City Blocks
BIRDIE: Lie-detector
BLITZER: Assassin
BODY-SHARKING: Illegal dealing in the bodies of living humans
BOING!: Miracle rubber
CITY BLOCK: Towering developments, housing over 50,000 citizens
DROKK: Local exclamation!
FATTIES: Obese citizens
FUTSIE: Person suffering from future-shock
GILA-MUNJA: Cursed Earth mutants used as assassins
GRUD: God
HONDO CITY: Japan
H-WAGON: Justice Department flying transport
I-BLOCK: Justice Department safe-house
ISO-CUBE: Individual cells, housed in high security prisons
JIMP: Judge impersonator
JUVES: Youngsters
JUVE CUBE: Similar to Iso-Cubes, for young offenders
LAWGIVER: Judge's multi-faceted gun
LAWMASTER: Judge's high-powered motorbike

LONG WALK: Judge retirement in the Cursed Earth
MO-PAD: Mobile home
MUTIE: Cursed Earth mutant
OZ: Australia
PERP: Perpetrator, criminal
PERP-RUNNING: Illegal transportation of wanted criminals
PLASTEEN: All-purpose building material
PSI-JUDGE: Judge with telepathic abilities
RADLANDS: Radioactive wasteland
RESYK: Human corpse recycling plant
ROOKIE: Judge in training
SCRAWLER: Graffiti artist
SECTOR HOUSE: Justice Department control station
SJS: Special Judicial Squad; Judge investigators
SOV-BLOCK: Formerly Russia, now East-Meg One and Two
STOOKIE-GLAND: Anti-aging drug. Illegal
STUB GUN: Hand-held laser rifle
STUMM GAS: Last-resort riot gas, sometimes fatal
UMPTY CANDY: Highly addictive sweet. Illegal
WALLY SQUAD: Undercover Judges

ROOKIE

CITY BLOCK

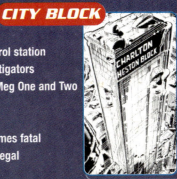

MEET JUDGE DREDD...

Mega-City One, a vast 22nd century metropolis stretching down the eastern seaboard of post-apocalyptic North America. Beyond its walls lies the radioactive wasteland known as the Cursed Earth. As crime in the hugely overpopulated Mega-City runs rampant, only the judges can prevent total anarchy. Empowered to dispense instant justice, they are judge, jury and executioner in one — and the most feared and respected of them all is Judge Dredd. He *is* the law!

PREVIOUSLY...

First introduced during the *Judge Child quest* (in Prog #162), Justice One is the Justice Department's primary space cruiser, used for interstellar travel to Mega-City One's various space colonies, prisoner transportation and routine patrols. Meanwhile, back in Mega-City One, the Judges have discredited a dissident group calling for democracy – but their voice has not yet been silenced…

JUDGE DREDD

JUSTICE ONE

PART 1

AT LAUNCH PAD J, SECTOR TWELVE SPACEPORT, THE JUSTICE DEPARTMENT STARSHIP *JUSTICE ONE* IS READIED FOR TAKEOFF ON A ROUTINE CIRCUIT TOUR OF MEGA-CITY ONE'S SPACE COLONIES.

THE MISSION WILL LAST FIVE WEEKS. A TEAM OF STREET JUDGES WILL TRAVEL WITH THE CREW TO CHECK ON LOCAL COLONY LAW ENFORCEMENT AND DEAL FORCIBLY WITH MAJOR INFRINGEMENTS OF GALACTIC LAW.

IT **SHOULD** BE NOTHING OUT OF THE ORDINARY. JUSTICE ONE AND HER CREW MAKE SEVERAL TRIPS LIKE THIS EVERY YEAR — BUT THIS TIME OUT, THINGS **WILL** BE DIFFERENT.

THIS TIME, WHAT HAPPENS ABOARD JUSTICE ONE WILL BE **UNIMAGINABLE**.

Script GARTH ENNIS
Art PETER DOHERTY
Lettering TOM FRAME

GOOD TO HAVE YOU ABOARD, JUDGE DREDD. THE COMPUTERS HAVE GOT HER ON HOLD WHILE YOUR BIKES ARE BEING STOWED AWAY.

THIS IS THE CREW — **REED'S** GUNNERY OFFICER, **LEWIS** IS CARGO CHIEF AND ALSO HANDLES ALIEN RELATIONS, AND **CARSON** HERE IS OUR NAVIGATOR.

AND THE ENGINEER.

HAWKINS IS JUST MAKING A FEW FINAL TOUCHES ON THE DRIVES. HE'S A BIT OF A PERFECTIONIST.

GOOD. I EXPECT THIS TRIP TO BE SMOOTH AND EFFICIENT, HAYES.

THAT GOES FOR THE REST OF YOU, TOO. I SEE NO POINT IN WASTING TIME, LET'S GET GOING.

I UNDERSTAND YOU'VE BEEN ABOARD BEFORE...?

CORRECT. THE JUDGE CHILD MISSION. *

JUDGES PROUDFOOT, LOGAN AND KINCAID ARE ALL NEW TO CIRCUIT DUTY, BUT THEY KNOW THE DRILL.

THE JUDGE CHILD...THAT'S ABOUT TEN YEARS BACK, ISN'T IT? WE'VE HAD A FEW CHANGES SINCE THEN.

I TOOK OVER FROM LARTER, ACTUALLY. THE SHIP'S BEEN REFITTED A COUPLE OF TIMES, JUST TO KEEP HER UP TO DATE WITH HEAVY CRUISERS LIKE THE FARGO AND THE SOLOMON.

HOW ABOUT THE CREW?

THEY'RE THE BEST.

* THARGNOTE: SEE PROGS 156-181.

LIGHT SPEED PLUS TEN, ALL SYSTEMS STEADY.

HYPERSPACE ACHIEVED.

NICE ONE. JUST SETTLE BACK AND ENJOY THE TRIP.

WRONG, HAYES.

I DON'T WANT YOU FLYBOYS GETTING **SLOPPY.** I'M ORDERING HOURLY SYSTEMS CHECKS — CARSON, YOU BEGIN. MEANTIME, REED AND LEWIS CAN SHOW ME ROUND THE SHIP.

WE'LL START WITH THE ARMAMENT. WHAT'S THE STATUS THERE, REED?

UH, STANDARD BLASTERS AND PROJECTILE CANNON, JUDGE DREDD. NUCLEAR PAYLOAD IN AUXILIARY BAYS.

PROUDFOOT, THIS IS DREDD. I WANT THE LAWMASTERS CHECKED FOR OUR FIRST PLANETFALL. YOU'VE GOT 17 HOURS.

WILCO, DREDD.

HAD A FEELING OLD STONEYFACE WOULD WORK US HARD ON THIS TRIP.

LIGHTEN UP, PROUDFOOT. IT WON'T BE HALF AS BAD AS HE'S WORKING THE **CREW.**

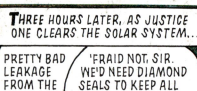

THREE HOURS LATER, AS JUSTICE ONE CLEARS THE SOLAR SYSTEM...

PRETTY BAD LEAKAGE FROM THE ENGINES, HAWKINS. NOTHING YOU CAN DO?

'FRAID NOT, SIR. WE'D NEED DIAMOND SEALS TO KEEP ALL THE COOLANT IN — BUT THE LEAKS JUST MESS THE PLACE UP A BIT. DOESN'T AFFECT PERFORMANCE.

OKAY. WHERE DO WE REFUEL THIS TRIP?

THERE'S A RENDEZVOUS ARRANGED WITH A TANKER, JUST OFF ALMEIRA...

UH, JUST A SECOND...

PROBLEMS?

SHOULDN'T BE...JUST WONDERING WHY THIS PANEL'S LEAKING LUBRICANT. THERE'S NO FEEDLINES UP THERE TO **LEAK**.

STRANGE...THIS ISN'T LUBRICANT. LOOKS MORE LIKE —

OH MY GRUD!

DROKK! PROUDFOOT!

NEXT PROG: **WHODUNNIT?**

JUDGE DREDD
JUSTICE ONE

PART 2

THREE HOURS OUT FROM EARTH, A SHOCK DISCOVERY INTERRUPTS THE COLONY SECURITY TOUR OF *JUSTICE ONE* —

THIS IS **DREDD.** I WANT ALL JUDGES AND CREW PERSONNEL TO REPORT TO THE ENGINE ROOM **IMMEDIATELY.**

WHAT'S THIS ABOUT, JUDGE DREDD? I'VE GOT A **STARSHIP** TO RUN —

WE CAN'T FIND PROUDFOOT, DREDD. HE'S NOT WITH THE BIKES.

I KNOW...

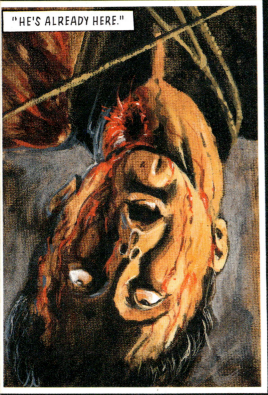

"HE'S ALREADY HERE."

HE WAS KILLED ABOUT AN HOUR AGO. HIS BODY WAS DRAGGED FROM THE SCENE AND HIDDEN. THAT CRAWLSPACE UP THERE HAS A BLOODTRAIL GOING DOWN IT.

I CHECKED THE COMPUTER JUST AFTER TAKEOFF. IT SHOWED NINE LIFE FORMS ABOARD — THE SEVEN OF YOU, ME, AND PROUDFOOT. NO-ONE HAS JOINED US SINCE, SO THAT JUST LEAVES ONE QUESTION...

WHICH ONE OF YOU KILLED HIM?

Script GARTH ENNIS
Art PETE DOHERTY
Lettering TOM FRAME

WHAT? ARE YOU CRAZY, DREDD?

I DON'T BELIEVE IT! JUDGE KILLING **JUDGE**?

IT WOULDN'T BE THE FIRST TIME, LOGAN.

AS OF NOW YOU ARE ALL UNDER SUSPICION. IT COULD BE ONE OR MORE OF YOU, BUT IT'S THE ONLY PLAUSIBLE EXPLANATION — SO THIS MISSION IS **OVER**.

JUST HOLD ON A MINUTE, HERE! WHAT DO YOU MEAN, IT'S OVER?

I MEAN I'M CANCELLING THE SECURITY TOUR, HAYES. THERE'S NO WAY WE CAN CONTINUE UNDER THESE CIRCUMSTANCES.

CARSON, WHERE'S THE NEAREST MEGA-CITY ONE OUTPOST?

UH, THAT WOULD BE THE DEEPBASE MISSILE SILOS OVER ON PLUTO, BUT IT MIGHT BE BETTER TO...

PLUTO IT IS.

EVERYONE HAND IN THEIR LAWGIVERS. CREW MEMBERS WILL CONTINUE RUNNING THE SHIP UNDER MY SUPERVISION. LOGAN AND KINCAID ARE CONFINED TO THEIR QUARTERS.

TELL ME ONE THING, DREDD. YOU'RE THE ONE GIVING ALL THE ORDERS...

HOW DO **WE** KNOW IT WASN'T **YOU**?

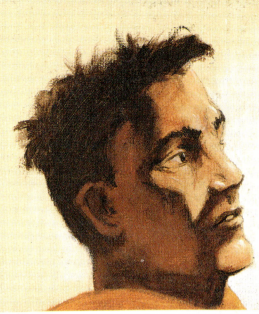

YOU'RE TALKING YOURSELF INTO TROUBLE, HAYES. SO FAR I'VE BEEN PRETTY PATIENT WITH YOU, BUT I'VE GOT A MURDERER TO FIND AND I **DON'T** HAVE TIME TO PLAY GAMES.

I'M SENIOR JUDGE HERE AND **I** KNOW I DIDN'T DO IT. THAT'S ALL THE REASON I NEED TO STOP THE MISSION. NOW GET BACK TO YOUR POST.

AREN'T YOU FORGETTING SOMETHING?

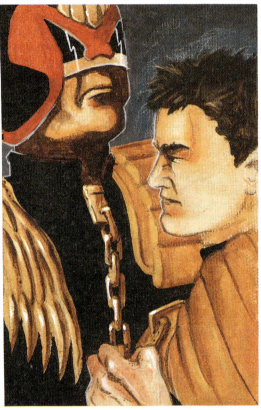

SAME GOES FOR THE REST OF YOU. LET'S HAVE 'EM.

SO WHO DID IT? AND WHY?

HE'D CHECKED THE PERSONNEL PROFILES THE NIGHT BEFORE — STANDARD PROCEDURE BEFORE TAKING COMMAND OF A SECURITY TOUR — AND NONE OF THEM LOOKED ANYTHING **LIKE** BEING UNSTABLE.

BUT THEN, THIS WAS TOTALLY UNHEARD OF, AND NORMAL RULES JUST DIDN'T APPLY.

I'M RIGGING THE DOOR TO THE SHIP'S ALARM SIREN — SO IF YOU TRY AND GET OUT, I'LL KNOW ABOUT IT.

THIS IS A BIT MUCH, DREDD —

IF YOU TURN OUT INNOCENT, LOGAN, YOU'LL HAVE MY APOLOGIES.

HE WAS PRETTY SURE IT WASN'T **KINCAID** OR **LOGAN**. THEY JUST WEREN'T THE TYPE. TOO YOUNG. BOTH JUST TWO YEARS OUT OF THE ACADEMY — NOT MANY JUDGES WENT BAD THAT QUICK.

NOT MANY JUDGES WENT BAD, PERIOD.

THE CREW...? **HAYES** HAD AN ATTITUDE PROBLEM, BUT SHIPCREW OFTEN DID — AND IT DIDN'T MAKE HIM A KILLER. THE OTHERS HE DIDN'T KNOW. **HAWKINS** SEEMED GENUINELY SHOCKED WHEN THEY'D FOUND THE CORPSE. **REED** AND **LEWIS** WERE WITH HIM ON THE SHIP INSPECTION ROUND ABOUT THE TIME OF THE MURDER...

BUT THAT DIDN'T STOP THEM BEING **INVOLVED** — AND BESIDES, HE ONLY HAD AN **APPROXIMATE** TIME OF DEATH.

THE TROUBLE WAS, OUT HERE IN SPACE THERE JUST WASN'T THE NECESSARY EQUIPMENT. HE'D NEED FORENSIC GEAR AND LIE DETECTORS — ALL JUDGES WERE TRAINED TO FOOL THE HAND-HELD UNITS.

PROUDFOOT'S LAWGIVER WAS MISSING FROM ITS HOLSTER — THE KILLER WOULD HAVE HANDED IT OVER INSTEAD OF THEIR OWN. SO THEY ANTICIPATED THE CORPSE BEING FOUND, GUESSED THEY'D HAVE TO TURN IN THEIR GUN — BUT THIS WAY THEY WERE STILL ARMED, AND WITH NO ACCESS TO **MAC***, HE COULDN'T CHECK THE SERIAL NUMBERS.

TRICKY CREEP...

***MAC** – JUSTICE DEPT MAINFRAME COMPUTER

THIS WAS WHERE PROUDFOOT HAD BEEN WORKING — AND IN ALL LIKELIHOOD IT WAS WHERE HE HAD **DIED**.

COURSE FOR PLUTO LOCKED, GRUD**DAMMIT**!

WHY COULDN'T YOU HAVE STOOD UP TO DREDD? MADE HIM CARRY ON WITH THE MISSION?

ME? WE WOULDN'T EVEN BE IN THIS MESS IF **YOU** HADN'T CUT PROUDFOOT'S THROAT...

WHAT THE DROKK **ELSE** WAS I SUPPOSED TO DO? HE'D FOUND THE MONEY — HE'D HAVE BLOWN THE WHOLE PLAN!

OKAY, TAKE IT EASY. NO POINT IN SQUABBLING... WHERE ARE THE OTHERS?

CHECKING THE BLASTER TUBES. THEY WON'T HEAR US.

SO WHAT ARE WE GOING TO DO? IF WE GET TO PLUTO, WE'RE **SUNK**.

YEAH... WE'VE GOT TO MAKE THAT RENDEZVOUS AT ALMEIRA OR WE'LL NEVER HAVE THE FUEL FOR OUR LITTLE TRIP. DREDD'LL BE CHECKING THE COMPUTER, SO WE CAN'T FOOL HIM INTO THINKING WE'RE HEADING FOR PLUTO WHILE GOING IN THE **OTHER** DIRECTION...

BEFORE WE ALTER COURSE, DREDD'S GOTTA **GO**.

TOO RIGHT! HE'S SNIFFING ROUND THE CARGO BAY, RIGHT WHERE I **KILLED** PROUDFOOT! I DIDN'T HAVE TIME TO MOVE OUR STUFF — HE'LL CATCH ON ANY SECOND!

RELAX...

THE ONLY THING DREDD'S GOING TO CATCH IS **LEAD POISONING**.

NOTHING TOO OBVIOUS... THE TOOLBOX WAS OPEN, SO HE'D ACTUALLY GOT DOWN TO WORK. THAT WAS NO REASON TO KILL HIM. HAD HE SEEN SOMETHING HE SHOULDN'T HAVE?

VISIBILITY WAS LOUSY IN THE CARGO BAY. IT WOULD HAVE BEEN CLOSE, WHATEVER IT WAS...

UNLESS HE WENT LOOKING. POWER LEVELS ON THE TOOLS WERE LOW. TO RECHARGE THEM HE'D HAVE GONE OVER TO THE POWER OUTLET...

SO MUCH FILTH ON THE WALL, YOU COULDN'T TELL WHAT WAS WHAT. SOME OF IT COULD BE BLOOD.

PROUDFOOT WOULDN'T HAVE GONE MESSING WITH A POWER OUTLET IN BAD LIGHT. MAYBE HE WENT TO FIND A TORCH...

THE DRAWER WAS LOOSE—

SOMETHING BEHIND IT... A CASE.

NOT EXACTLY REGULATION ISSUE ON A JUSTICE DEPARTMENT CRAFT. WHY CIVILIAN CLOTHES?

AND WHY KILL TO COVER IT UP?

VERY SMART, DREDD... BUT IN JUST ONE SECOND IT WON'T MATTER A DAMN!

NEXT PROG: BATTLE STATIONS!

DROKK!

As JUSTICE ONE heads for Pluto, the mystery killer on board tries to put the zap on **JUDGE DREDD**.

Script — G. Ennis
Art — P. Doherty
Lettering — T. Frame

GRUD ALMIGHTY! HE'S **FAST**!

I'M SWITCHING TO **HEATSEEKERS**, SCUMBAG! **GIVE IT UP**!

WHAT THE HELL DO I DO NOW? HE'S TOO GOOD FOR ME!

GOTTA GET AWAY —

WHAT'S ALL THE SHOOTING — OH MY **GRUD**!

YOU!

SORRY, REED—

EEARRGHH!

BUT YOU JUST SAW TOO MUCH!

STOMM!

DID YOU SEE HIM, REED? WHO WAS IT?

UUUHH...HE'S KILLED...ME...

HE...UNH...LOOKED ME... RIGHT IN...THE...EYES...

H...UHHH...

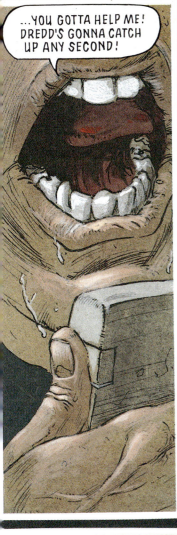

...YOU GOTTA HELP ME! DREDD'S GONNA CATCH UP ANY SECOND!

GRUD, HE'S OUT FOR BLOOD!

ALERT! ALERT! BULKHEAD DOORS SEALING!

JEEZ—

HOLD IT, CREEP!

KRUNNGG

OVERRIDE'S JAMMED—

HAVE TO IMPROVISE!

KINCAID AND LOGAN—

YOU TWO ARE OFFICIALLY INNOCENT! GET YOUR LAWGIVERS FROM MY CABIN AND MEET ME ON THE BRIDGE!

HE'S THROUGH THE DOORS—HE'LL BE HERE ANY MINUTE! GRUD! HE'S BOUND TO KNOW IT WAS YOU!

OH, JEEZ—I GOTTA DITCH THIS!

WHAT IN GRUD'S NAME—?

LEWIS!

SKIP, WHAT'S GOING ON? I THOUGHT DREDD IMPOUNDED ALL THE GUNS?

NOT THIS ONE! CATCH, LEWIS!

ZEE ZEE ZEE

THAT'S A PROXIMITY ALERT, DREDD! RADAR'S PICKED UP ANOTHER SHIP!

CHECK IT. AND NO TRICKS!

UM... I SHOW FOUR CONTACTS, RANGE SIX POINT NINE. ONE IS STABLE, THE OTHERS ARE CLOSING ON IT —

MAYDAY! MAYDAY! THIS IS THE STAR FREIGHTER ANDORRA, CALLING ANYONE IN RANGE! WE ARE UNDER ATTACK!

I REPEAT, WE ARE UNDER ATTACK! PIRATES JUMPED US JUST AS WE CLEARED THE SYSTEM — MUST'VE BEEN TRAILING US! THE MAIN DRIVES ARE DOWN — LIFE SUPPORT'S FAILING!

PLEASE ASSIST!

HELLLLLP!

DROKK! JUST WHAT WE DON'T NEED! OKAY, GET TO YOUR POSTS. I'LL HANDLE FIRE CONTROL NOW REED'S DEAD — BUT I KNOW ONE OF YOU IS THE KILLER AND BELIEVE ME THE MINUTE I SMELL A RAT, I SHOOT TO KILL!

NOW LET'S DO IT!

BATTLE STATIONS!

NEXT PROG: TORPEDOES AWAY!

JUDGE DREDD

JUSTICE ONE

PART 4

ON THE EDGE OF THE SOLAR SYSTEM, JUDGE DREDD IS ON THE POINT OF UNMASKING THE MURDERER ABOARD JUSTICE ONE. JUST THEN, A DISTRESS CALL COMES IN FROM THE FREIGHTER **ANDORRA** —

ONE MORE PASS AN' WE'LL BOARD HER, LADS!

AIM FOR JUST BEHIND THE BRIDGE, RIGHT? SEE IF YOU CAN KNOCK OUT THE POWER.

HOLD IT!

WHADDAYAMEAN, **HOLD IT?** WE'RE KINDA BUSY!

RADAR'S SHOWIN' A NEW CONTACT, SARGE! UNKNOWN VESSEL JUST DROPPED OUTTA HYPERSPACE, CLOSIN' FAST!

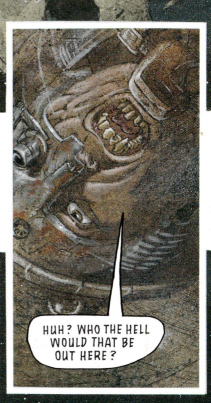

HUH? WHO THE HELL WOULD THAT BE OUT HERE?

BLACKBEARD'S SPUTUM! IT'S THE LAW!

Script G. Ennis
Art P. Doherty
Lettering T. Frame

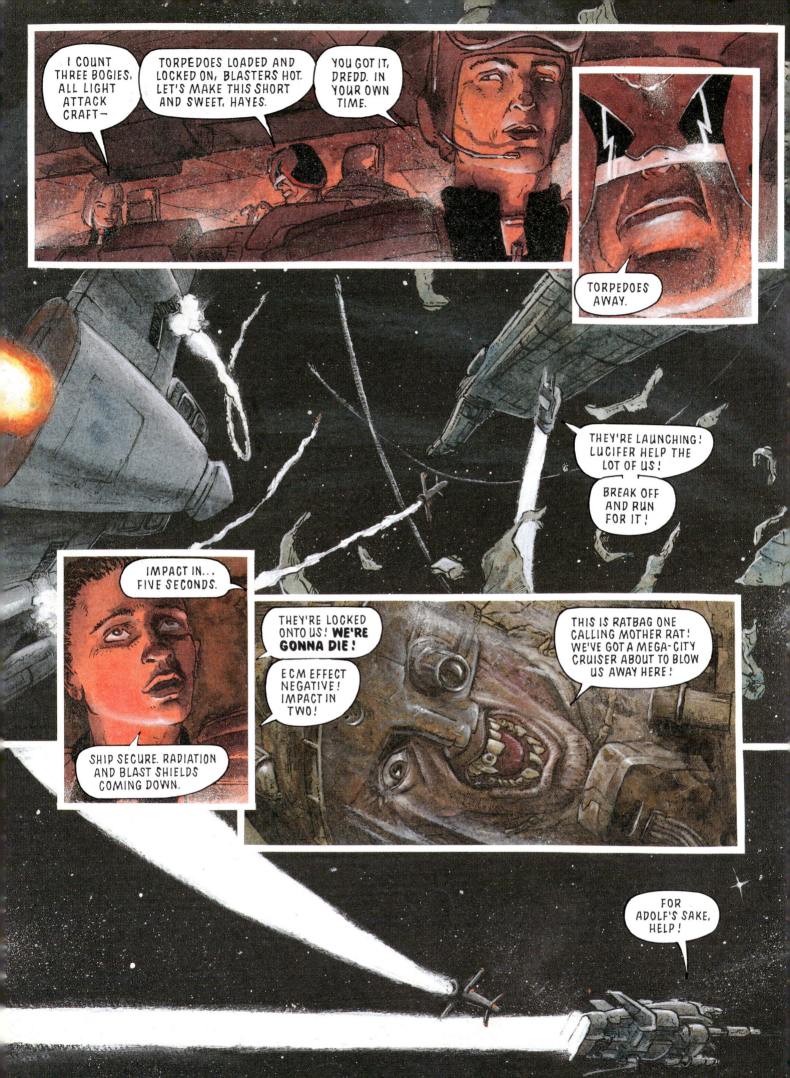

INITIAL DAMAGE REPORTS NEGATIVE. SHIELDS HOLDING.

STILL WITH US, HAWKINS?

YES SIR! ENGINES ARE FINE, NO COMPLAINTS.

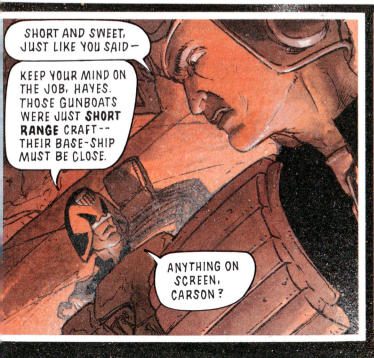

SHORT AND SWEET, JUST LIKE YOU SAID—

KEEP YOUR MIND ON THE JOB, HAYES. THOSE GUNBOATS WERE JUST **SHORT RANGE** CRAFT-- THEIR BASE-SHIP MUST BE CLOSE.

ANYTHING ON SCREEN, CARSON?

JUST US AND THE FREIGHTER, DREDD.

CHECK AGAIN. THEY COULD BE CLOAKED.

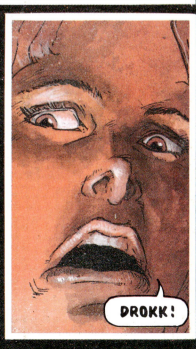

DROKK!

NEXT PROG: ADRIFT WITH A MURDERER...

SOUNDS LIKE THE ROBOTS WORKED.

I ONLY HEARD TWO SCREAMS... DREDD AND LEWIS MUST BE SOMEWHERE ELSE ON BOARD.

DROIDS TO **PURSUIT MODE** —

DOORS ARE FINE... LOOK, DREDD, YOU **CAN'T** THINK IT WAS ME! HAYES THREW ME THE GUN!

CALM DOWN, LEWIS. THERE'LL BE A FULL INVESTIGATION WHEN WE REACH PLUTO. IF YOU'RE INNOCENT THEN YOU'VE NOTHING TO WORRY ABOUT.

UNTIL THEN, I TRUST **NOBODY**.

FINISH OFF HERE AND LET'S GO.

OKAY, OKAY. KEEP YOUR HELMET ON, DREDD.

WHAT IN HELL—? NO!

AAAHHH!

GRUD **DAMMIT!**

YOU IN THERE! COME OUT WITH YOUR HANDS HIGH OR I OPEN FIRE!

OH, **SWELL**.

NEXT PROG: **THE REASON WH**

STOMM!

ABOARD *JUSTICE ONE*, THE MURDERERS CARSON AND HAYES HAVE WIPED OUT THE ENTIRE CREW. NOW ONLY ONE OBSTACLE REMAINS TO THEIR ESCAPE — *JUDGE DREDD*.

BACK **OFF**, TINHEAD!

RIVARIVARIVA

RIVETS, HUH?

YOU'RE OUTGUNNED, CREEPS!

FADDAM!

BIKE CANNON!

MY GRUD! HE'S GOT THREE OF THEM!

I'M CUTTING THIS **SHORT**!

JUDGE DREDD

PART **6**

JUSTICE ONE

YOU'RE CRAZY, DREDD! THE INSTANT WE BRING UP THE TURBINES YOU'LL BE SPLATTERED ALL OVER THE SHIP!

JUST **TRY IT**, HAYES!

COME ON, DREDD — BE **REASONABLE**! WE'VE BEEN PLANNING THIS FOR TWO YEARS — WE'VE HAD A **BELLYFUL** OF SHUTTLING SECURITY TOURS ROUND THE GALAXY! WE'RE GOING TO TAKE THE SHIP AND START LIVES OF OUR **OWN**!

WE'LL PAY YOU! WE'VE BUILT UP TWO HUNDRED GRAND FOR THIS TRIP — GIVE US SAFE PASSAGE AND IT'S ALL YOURS!

I'VE HEARD GARBAGE LIKE THAT BEFORE, HAYES! THE ONLY THING BENT JUDGES GET FROM ME IS A **BULLET**!

THREE SECONDS TO GIVE IT UP!

GO FOR IT!

NO—

YOUR MISTAKE, CREEP!

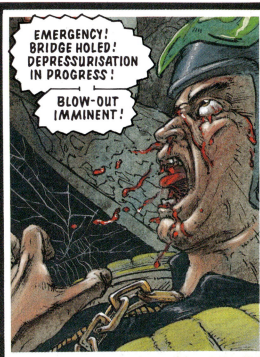

STRUCTURE'S INTACT. GUESS THEY DON'T BUILD 'EM LIKE HER ANYMORE.

LET'S HOPE PLUTO'S IN RANGE...

THIS IS JUSTICE ONE CALLING DEEPBASE PLUTO. JUSTICE ONE TO PLUTO. ARE YOU RECEIVING? OVER.

BZZZZZT-ING YOU, JUSTICE ONE. BAD TRZZZZZZMISSION. GO AHEAD. OVER.

THIS IS **JUDGE DREDD**. THE SHIP IS DAMAGED AND ADRIFT OUT ON THE SYSTEM RIM. THERE'S A CRIPPLED FREIGHTER IN THE SECTOR -- THEY'LL GIVE YOU OUR ROUGH CO-ORDINATES.

COULD DO WITH A PICK-UP BEFORE OXYGEN RUNS OUT.

KRRKZZZZT- COMPLYING. SHUTTLE ON ITZZZKKZT — HOME IN ON YOU FROM THE FREIGHTER.

WHZZZKKK ON OUT THERE?

MUTINY, MURDER, ATTEMPTED THEFT OF A JUSTICE DEPT VESSEL... I'LL GIVE YOU A FULL REPORT WHEN I GET IN. AND DON'T LEAVE IT TOO LONG, HUH? DREDD OUT.

CREEPS GO BAD, WIPE OUT A WHOLE SHIPCREW AND THREE JUDGES, THEN TRY TO STEAL A BATTLECRUISER...

LIVES OF THEIR OWN, HUH?

NOT WHILE I'M AROUND.

THE END

NEXT PROG: **THE KOOLE KILLER**

NEIGHBOURS GOT A BIT SUSPICIOUS WHEN THEY HEARD HIM SCREAMING, JUST BEFORE THE GRINDERS STARTED. THEY CALLED US.

GOT AN I.D?

YEAH, THE FINGERPRINTS ARE INTACT. DEFINITELY THE OCCUPANT.

TALKBACK

JUDGE DREDD

ONE **COOL JOHNNY COOL** BY NAME. DEEJAY WITH RADIO RADIO RADIO. CAUSE OF DEATH... WELL, KIND OF OBVIOUS, REALLY.

YEAH...

Script **GARTH ENNIS**
Art **GLENN FABRY**
Lettering **TOM FRAME**

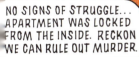

NO SIGNS OF STRUGGLE... APARTMENT WAS LOCKED FROM THE INSIDE. RECKON WE CAN RULE OUT MURDER.

HOW ABOUT SUICIDE?

HE COMES HOME... MAKES HIMSELF A CUP OF SYNTHI-CAFF ALL NICE AND CALM... **THEN** TAKES A HEADER DOWN THE GARBAGE GRINDER?

YOU DON'T FIND MANY SUICIDES DONE ON THE SPUR OF THE MOMENT LIKE THAT, SIMONSON.

CONTROL, THIS IS DREDD. GET A **PSI** OVER TO BRUNO BROOKES BLOCK.

ROG. PALMER'S ON STANDBY — ON HIS WAY.

SOON –

UMMM... JUDGE DREDD?

PALMER? WE GOT ONE FOR YOU, SON. GET TO WORK.

HIM? HOW CAN I GET RESIDUALS OFF –

WE SCRAPED HIS TOP HALF OUT OF THE GRINDER PIPES. YOU SHOULD FIND WHAT YOU NEED IN THERE.

OKAY, WE FIGURE THIS BIT IS WHAT'S LEFT OF THE BRAIN – THAT SHOULD BE THE FRONTAL LOBES, IF YOU WANT TO WORK YOUR WAY BACK FROM THERE. GOOD LUCK.

SEE PSI-DIV ARE ON FORM, AS USUAL. WHAT A GREENIE...

PALMER REACHES OUT WITH HIS MIND, SEARCHING, PROBING... MAKING CONTACT WITH THE ECHOES OF THE DEAD MAN'S LAST THOUGHTS...

EEEAAAHH!

PALMER!

PALMER! PALMER! WHAT IS IT?

MED UNIT TO LUX APT FOUR TWO, BROOKES BLOCK! PALMER IS DOWN!

TH-TH-TH-THE –

THE WHAT, PALMER? WHAT'S IN THERE?

THE H-H-

THE HATE-

THE STORY BEHIND [P]ALMER'S EXPERIENCE — [A]ND COOL JOHNNY [C]OOL'S UNPLEASANT [D]EMISE — BEGAN [S]EVERAL DAYS [E]ARLIER...

GOOOOD MORNING, MEGA-CITY ONE! **COOL JOHNNY COOL** BOPPIN' ATCHA WITH RADIO RADIO RADIO! TWENTY-FOUR HOUR RED-HOT MEGA **FUNK**!

YOU GOT IT, PEOPLOIDS! THE COOLEST DUDE IN ALL OF COOLDOM IS ON THE WAVES!

BEEPEEP BEEPEEP

AND STRAIGHTAWAY WE GOT US A CALLER! WHO'S THAT CALLING THE KING OF COOL?

ER...IT'S, UM, MR HESITANT, AH, COOL JOHNNY...

HA HA HA! WHAT A WILD AND CRAZY GUY! WHAT YOU GOT FOR US, HESITANT?

ER...AH...UMM...

BYE BYE, HESITANT! HAHAHA! HE'S HESITANT, THAT GUY, HE REALLY IS!

OKAY, PEOPLES — TIME FOR THE CAKESHAKIN', BOOGLESHOOGLIN' **NOISE**! STRAIGHT IN AT SIX ON THE CEE RAP CHART, HERE'S M.C. JACKJERK NO-TUNE AND DEEJAY RAWKUS WITH "WE STOLE THE BASSLINE"!

SO **HIT IT**!

YO, LADY! THE COOL ONE IS OFF ON VACATION — THAT'S **BOWEL** VACATION, BABE! BACK IN FIVE!

SNAP!

[U]NFORTUNATELY FOR THE COOLEST [D]UDE IN ALL OF COOLDOM, THE [R]ADIO RADIO RADIO CONVENIENCES [A]RE IN URGENT NEED OF A LITTLE **MAINTENANCE** —

MC WC

AAAARRGH!

UUUNNNH... UNCOOL, MAN...

BUT YOU CAN'T KEEP A GOOD CRETIN DOWN, AND AFTER A QUICK VISIT TO A MED UNIT, COOL JOHNNY COOL WAS BACK...

GET **WITH IT**, BABES AND BABELETS! COOL JOHNNY COOL OUT OF TRACTION, BACK IN ACTION – AIN'T NO **LOO** CAN KEEP ME FROM **YOU**!

BEEPEEP BEEPEEP

WHO'S THAT ON THE LINE FOR THE UNK OF FUNK?

HEY, **COOL JOHNNY COOL**... WHY DON'T YOU **GO FRY**!

ER... SAY AGAIN, CALLER...?

I **MEAN IT**, COOL JOHNNY COOL. WHY DON'T YOU DROP **DEAD** – OR BETTER YET, JUMP OUT OF THE **WINDOW**!

WHAT IN GRUD'S NAME IS HE DOING?

JOHNNY, **STOP**! WE'RE TEN FLOORS UP, YOU JERK!

WHAT'S **WRONG** WITH YOU, JOHNNY?

UH... THE DUDE ON THE PHONE TOLD COOL JOHNNY TO DO IT, BABELET, DIDN'T YOU HEAR?

WHAT? THE GUY WAS PHONING ABOUT YOUR RAPATTACK **QUIZ**, JOHNNY! WHAT ARE YOU **ON**?

QUIZ...? THAT'S NOT WHAT THIS DUDE LOBED...

DIDN'T **YOU** HEAR HIM, MY MAN? HE TOLD THE PRINCE OF ALL CATS TO GO FRY... TO **DROP DEAD**! YOU MUST'VE HEARD HIM!

NOT ME, COOL JOHNNY! IT WAS ABOUT THE QUIZ!

WEIRD!

SORRY ABOUT THE DELAY, FUNKFANS — LITTLE UNCOOL ACTIVITY THERE FOR THE MAN YOU ALL **LURRRVE!**

BUT LET'S FORGET THE BAD AN' START GETTIN' **RAD!** YOU GOT RADIO RADIO RADIO BEAMIN' ATCHA WITH THE HOTTEST —

YOU GOT **ANY IDEA** HOW **ANNOYING** YOU ARE, COOL JOHNNY COOL?

SNAP!

COOOO

HUH?

ON AND ON AND **ON**, DRONING AWAY WITH YOUR **STUPID** VOICE, **NEVER** SHUTTING UP!

WE ALL **HATE** YOU, COOL JOHNNY COOL!

YOU'RE A TOTAL SLIMEBALL, COOL JOHNNY COOL! YOU'VE BEEN GETTING RIGHT UP OUR NOSES FOR FAR TOO LONG, COOL JOHNNY COOL!

HOW ABOUT YOU JUST OFF YOURSELF AND BRIGHTEN UP OUR WHOLE DAY, COOL JOHNNY COOL? HOW ABOUT IT?

YEAH! GO ON! END IT ALL! YOU'VE NO IDEA HOW MUCH WE HATE YOU, COOL JOHNNY COOL!

KILL YOURSELF!

FOR SOME REASON, COOL JOHNNY COOL SPENDS HIS DAY ATTEMPTING TO FOLLOW THIS UNFRIENDLY ADVICE...

FLOOSH!

GLUG-GLUBBLE-GLUG-!

JEEZ! JOHNNY!

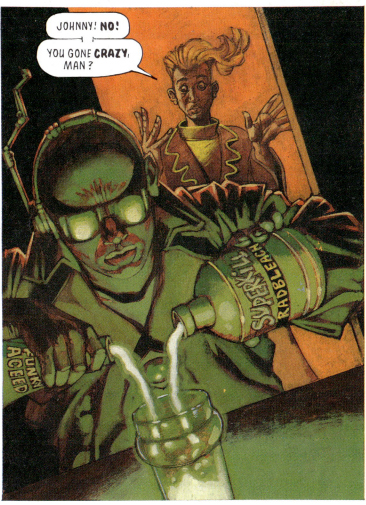

JOHNNY! **NO!**

YOU GONE **CRAZY,** MAN?

LOOK, JOHNNY, YOU'RE OBVIOUSLY UNDER A LOT OF STRESS. NOBODY ELSE HEARS THESE **VOICES** YOU KEEP TALKING ABOUT — IT'S ALL IN YOUR **HEAD**.

BUT...BUT...

YOU BETTER TAKE SOME TIME OFF, JOHNNY. — SEE A DOCTOR, HUH? CAN'T HAVE OUR TOP DEEJAY GOING OFF THE RAILS.

HEAD BUCKCAT

AND SO, COOL JOHNNY RETURNS HOME. BUT THE VOICES AREN'T FINISHED WITH HIM YET...

BUMMER, BABE! **TOTAL** COOLNESS DEFICIENCY!

PAL SWEE PAD

WE'RE STILL **HERE**, COOL JOHNNY COOL!

AAAAH!

WHAT **IS** THIS, MAN? WHY ARE THESE UNFUNKY VOICES HASSLING THE DUKE OF DEF?

BECAUSE YOU'RE AN **ANNOYING LITTLE TWERP**, COOL JOHNNY COOL!

EVER FANCIED SWALLOWING A COUPLE OF **RAZOR BLADES**, COOL JOHNNY COOL? GO ON, **DO IT!**

BUT-BUT **WHY**? WHY ARE YOU **DOING** THIS? WHAT DO YOU **WANT**?

BECAUSE WE THINK YOU'RE AN IRRITATING, BORING, USELESS PIECE OF TRASH, COOL JOHNNY COOL!

WE WANT YOU TO **KILL** YOURSELF, COOL JOHNNY COOL!

TELL YOU WHAT, HOW ABOUT YOU JUST THROW YOURSELF DOWN THE GRUDDAM GARBAGE GRINDER, COOL JOHNNY COOL!

AND HE DID JUST THAT. THE VERDICT...

IT WAS EVERYONE.

HE...HE MUST HAVE BEEN...MUST HAVE HAD A LATENT PSI-TALENT. COOL WAS A **PSI**. HE STARTED PICKING UP EMANATIONS FROM THE WHOLE **CITY**, DREDD. **EVERYONE** IN MEGA-CITY HATED THE GUY — AND ALL OF A SUDDEN HE COULD **FEEL** IT.

AND IT WAS SO STRONG IT KILLED HIM.

THE TECHS AT RADIO RADIO RADIO SAY COOL HAD AN ACCIDENT A FEW DAYS AGO — GOT A BAD KNOCK ON THE HEAD. COULD THAT HAVE WOKEN HIS PSI-POWER?

YEAH. YEAH, IT COULD.

THIS IS A TAPE OF HIS LAST SHOW, PALMER. RADIO RADIO RADIO SENT IT OVER. MIGHT GIVE YOU A HINT.

ALL THOSE PEOPLE, DREDD — **MILLIONS** OF THEM. THEY KILLED HIM JUST BY THINKING ABOUT HIM, AND THEY DIDN'T EVEN KNOW THEY WERE DOING IT...

WHY? WHAT WAS SO **BAD** ABOUT COOL JOHNNY COOL?

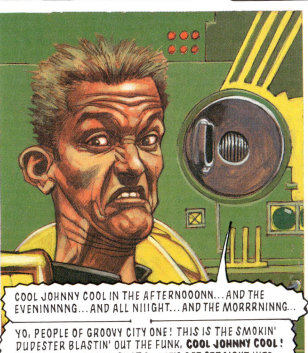

COOL JOHNNY COOL IN THE AFTERNOOONN...AND THE EVENINNNNG...AND ALL NIIIGHT...AND THE MORRRNINNG...

YO, PEOPLE OF GROOVY CITY ONE! THIS IS THE SMOKIN' DUDESTER BLASTIN' OUT THE FUNK, **COOL JOHNNY COOL**! AM I **HOT** OR ARE YOU **SNOT**? LET'S GET STRAIGHT INTO THE CHARTS — **NO**! LET'S **NOT**! LET'S TALK FOR A WHILE ABOUT **ME**! I'M THE GOD OF COOL, THE BUDDHA OF —

GRUD! I HOPE THE LITTLE CREEP **ROTS IN HELL**!

NEXT PROG: **ANY OLD IRON?**

WITNESSES SAY THIS GUY WALKED RIGHT UP TO TRAVIANO AND EXPLODED...

EX-MAN. GOTTA BE.

YEAH. YOU CHECK OUT TRAVIANO'S ENEMIES, CAGNEY -- I'LL TAKE THE EX-MEN.

CREEPS ARE **DUE** A **SLAPPING** DOWN.

EX(PLOSIVE)-MEN WERE A RECENT ARRIVAL ON THE BIG MEG CRIME SCENE. THEY WERE THE MEN WITH **NOTHING TO LOSE.**

DR J. QUACK

OH GRUD, NO! NOT -- NOT THE BLACK PUKE!

'FRAID SO, CITIZEN MEET. **TERMINAL.**

B-B-BUT I'VE GOT A **FAMILY!** HOW WILL **MOANA** AND LITTLE **DURK** SURVIVE WITHOUT ME?

I THINK YOU MIGHT HAVE WHAT IT TAKES TO BE AN **EX-MAN,** CITIZEN MEET...

BE AT THIS ADDRESS, MIDNIGHT.

AND, LATER --

DURK WUV OO, DADDY!

DADDY LOVES YOU TOO, LITTLE DURK!

AND TONIGHT DADDY'S GONNA **BLOW** HIMSELF TO KINGDOM **DROKK** FOR YOU, LITTLE DURK...

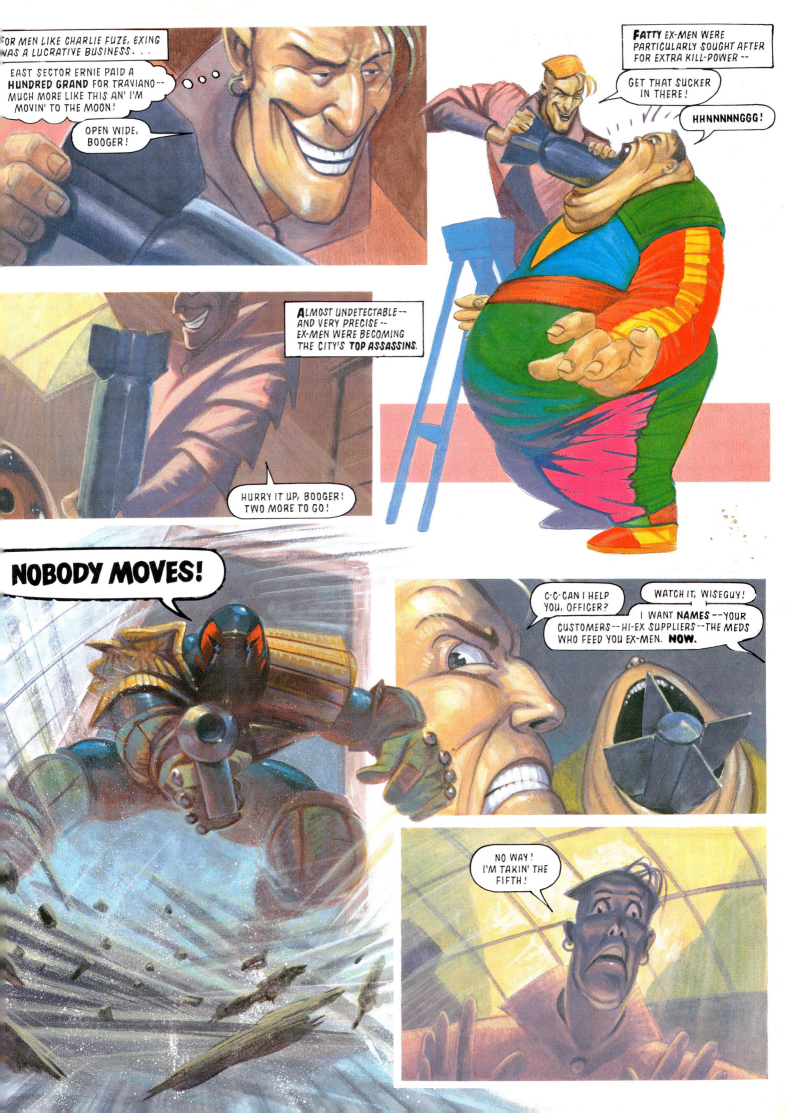

WHAT FIFTH? THIS CREEP'S FINISHED, CONTROL-- BUT HE'S GOT AN EX-MAN WORKING TONIGHT. I NEED AN H-WAGON TO LE GORB HI-DINER. IMMEDIATE.

GRUD! ONE-FORTY'S CRUISING THE SECTOR LINE -- ON THEIR WAY!

STAFF AT THE FLOATING RESTAURANT ARE SWIFTLY INFORMED --

WE'RE GONNA DIE!

AN EX-HOMME! WHERE IS HE?

IL COULD BE ANYONE!

BETTER GET IT OVER WITH...

LE GORB IN SIGHT, DREDD!

ER... SPITGUN MCCOY? I'M-I'M AN EX-MAN...

MON DROKK! C'EST DREDD!

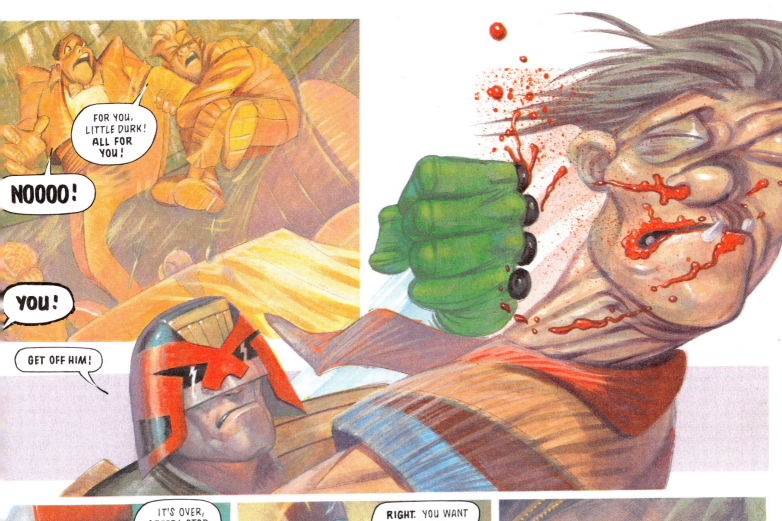

AW NO! I SCREWED UP! I'M **SORRY**, LITTLE DURK!

DADDY LOVES Y-

WH-WHO'S LITTLE DURK?

WHO CARES?

BUT THE LAW CANNOT BE EVERYWHERE AT ONCE... AND THERE ARE PLENTY MORE TERMINAL CASES WILLING TO TAKE UP **EXING**...

HEH HEH HEH! WITH TRAVIANO OUTTA THE PICTURE, THE WHOLE EAST SECTOR RACKETS ARE MINE FOR THE TAKING!

EAST SECTOR ERNIE?

I'M AN **EX-MAN**.

THE EN

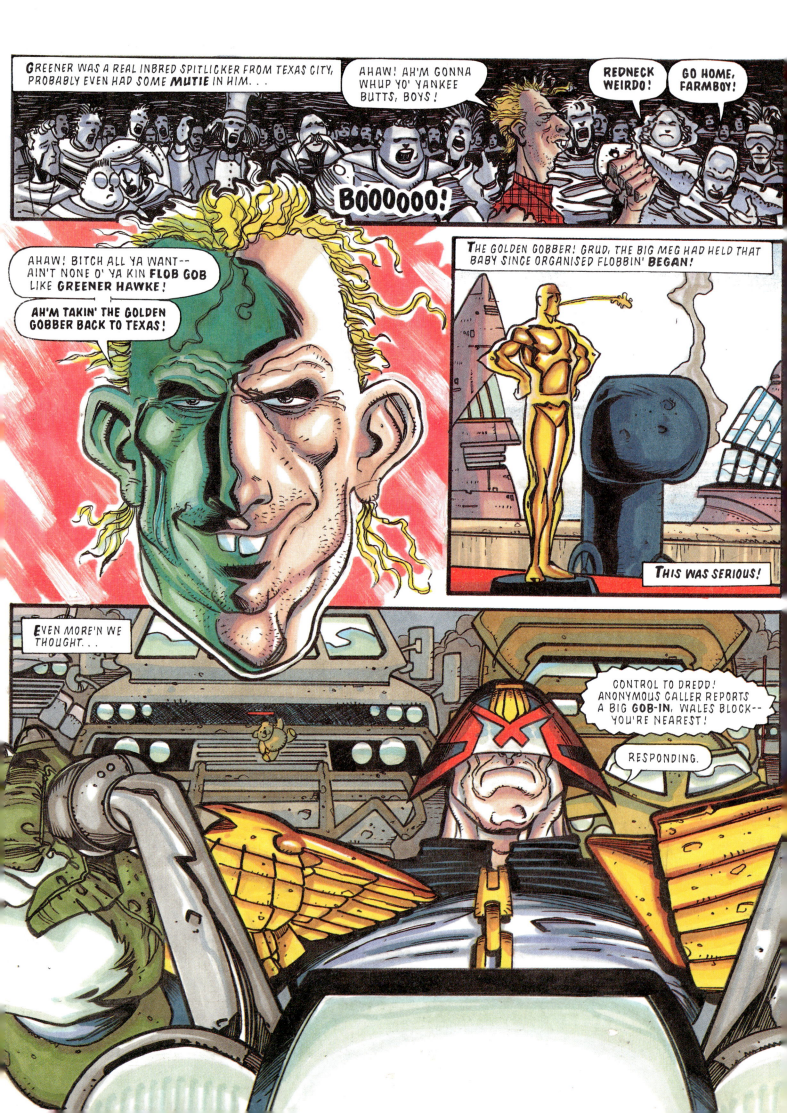

JUDGE DREDD

TWILIGHT'S LAST GLEAMING

MAJOR!

Script **G. ENNIS**
Art **J. BURNS**
Lettering **T. FRAME**

MEGA-CITY ONE, NOVEMBER 2113...

REFERENDUM DAY.

DON'T MOVE, MAJOR. WE—

RELAX, DEKKER.

MAJOR TOOK THE EASY WAY OUT.

MMM.

RILEY CALLED THROUGH — GRICE SQUEALED ON HIS WAY TO THE TITAN SHUFFLE.

THE FOURTH TRAITOR IS **WINDSOR**, AND THEIR CONTACT IN CONTROL IS YOUR OLD PAL **DEGAULLE**. GOT 'EM ON HOLD DOWNSTAIRS.

ON MY WAY.

CONTROL — DREDD. MAJOR'S COMMITTED SUICIDE. BETTER GET A CLEAN-UP CREW DOWN HERE.

THAT'S A ROJ, DREDD.

YOU'RE WASHED UP, DEGAULLE. YOUR CO-CONSPIRATORS ARE ALL DEAD OR ON THE TITAN TRIP — YOU'RE NEXT. WANT TO TELL ME ABOUT ANYONE ELSE INVOLVED IN THE PLOT AGAINST ME, OR DO WE USE THE PENTATHOL?

DAMN YOU, DREDD! YOU'RE ENJOYING THIS!

I'M IN NO MOOD FOR YOUR BULL, DEGAULLE! WHO ELSE?

N-N-NO-ONE!

THERE'S NO-ONE, DREDD. WE COULDN'T TRUST THEM — THEY'RE ALL READY TO HAND THIS CITY TO THE DEMOCRATS IN THE REFERENDUM, JUST LIKE YOU.

THE FOOLS!

LIE DETECTOR CONFIRMS, DREDD. SHE'S THE LAST.

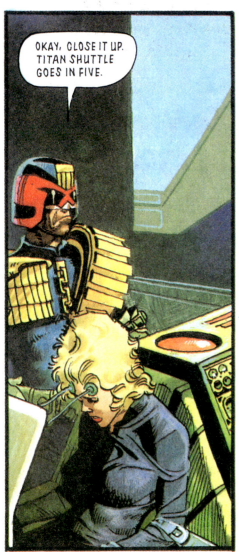

OKAY, CLOSE IT UP. TITAN SHUTTLE GOES IN FIVE.

I DON'T GET IT, DEGAULLE. WE MAY HAVE HAD OUR DIFFERENCES, BUT I ALWAYS THOUGHT YOU WERE A DAMN GOOD JUDGE. WHY THROW IT DOWN THE TOILET?

WHY-? HA!

BECAUSE I'M NOT A GRUDDAM ROBOT, DREDD!

FIFTEEN YEARS I'M ON THE STREETS — THEN SOME LITTLE PUNK TAKES HALF MY GUTS OUT WITH A LAS-BLASTER AND I WIND UP STUCK BEHIND A SCREEN IN CONTROL!

AND I JUST CAN'T STOP THINKING, JEEZ GRUP ABOVE — IS THIS ALL I GET OUT OF IT?

'IS THIS ALL I GET OUT OF IT...'

CONTROL, WE'RE FINISHED HERE. INFORM THE CHIEF JUDGE I'M ON MY WAY.

WILCO.

HE'D TAKEN THE **HIKE** BECAUSE OF IT.

A YOUNG JUVE ASKED HIM QUESTIONS HE COULD FIND NO ANSWERS FOR, AND WHEN THE KID DIED DREDD FELT RESPONSIBLE FOR **ALL** OF IT.

INTERROGATION CUBES

THAT WASN'T THE POINT. IT HADN'T CROSSED HIS MIND ONCE, NOT IN HIS TIME OF DOUBT, NOR WHEN THE CURSED EARTH STRETCHED BEFORE HIM, OLD SILVER'S "FAREWELL, DREDD" ECHOING IN HIS EARS — NOR WHEN HE WALKED AS A DEAD MAN, COMING BACK TO SAVE HIS CITY FROM NECROPOLIS.

NO, HIS PROBLEM HAD BEEN **DIFFERENT.**

RESPONSIBLE FOR A CITY WHERE FREEDOM WAS BOUND IN CHAINS OF IRON, AND JUSTICE WAS BUT A TINY FLICKER IN THE COLD, HARD LIGHT OF THE LAW.

WHERE THE JUDGES STAMPED ON PEOPLE WHO ASKED — PEACEFULLY — FOR NOTHING MORE THAN THE RIGHT TO DETERMINE THEIR OWN DESTINY.

AND YES, HE WAS RESPONSIBLE, JUST AS MUCH AS ANYONE WHO WORE THE EAGLE OF JUSTICE IN MEGA-CITY ONE.

BUT TO FEEL **GUILT**...TO FEEL GUILT WAS TO THINK LIKE A MAN, NOT A JUDGE.

BECAUSE WHERE A MAN WOULD BE WEAK, A JUDGE WOULD BE STRONG. WHERE A MAN WOULD FOOL HIMSELF THAT MILLIONS OF PEOPLE COULD LIVE TOGETHER IN PEACE, A JUDGE WOULD KNOW THAT THAT WAS JUST A PIPEDREAM, AND THAT IRON-FISTED **LAW** WAS NEEDED TO STOP MURDEROUS **CHAOS**.

AND MORE THAN ANYTHING ELSE, **DREDD WAS A JUDGE.**

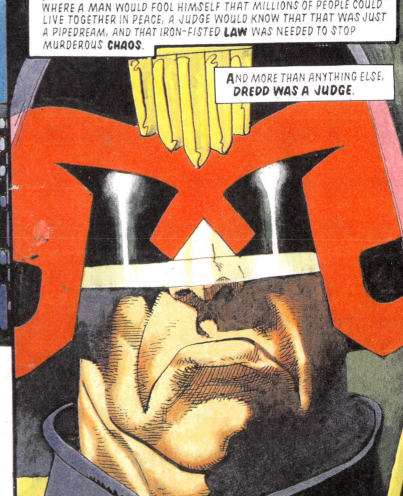

HE DIDN'T **NEED** ANYTHING OUT OF IT. THE JOB WAS ITS OWN REWARD.

155
TOP FLOOR

THIRTEEN YEARS AGO HE'D BEEN RETURNING FROM HIS TOUR AS JUDGE MARSHAL OF LUNA-ONE, AND AS THEY WERE COMING IN ON THE SPACEPORT HE'D GLANCED OUT OF THE WINDOW.

FROM THAT HIGH UP THE CITY LOOKED BEAUTIFUL, LIKE A HUGE JEWEL ON THE EAST COAST — SUN DANCING ON THE GLASSEEN TOWERS, THE MEGA-WAYS CRISS-CROSSING IN A BLUR OF MOVEMENT, AND A MUTED NEON GLOW WINKING FROM THE CONSTANT TWILIGHT OF THE LOWEST LEVELS.

HOWDY, JOE. GLAD YOU COULD JOIN US.

HALF AN HOUR TO GO.

YEAH.

HE COULDN'T SEE THE **CANCER** FROM THAT DISTANCE, THE BLOATED EVIL **ROT** THAT TOUCHED EVERYONE BELOW AND CUT A FLAW IN THE JEWEL LIKE A GANGRENOUS WOUND.

BUT DREDD LOOKED OUT OVER THE CITY — **HIS** CITY — AND HE **KNEW.**

"MEGA-CITY ONE...EIGHT HUNDRED MILLION PEOPLE AND EVERYONE OF THEM A POTENTIAL **CRIMINAL.** THE MOST VIOLENT, EVIL CITY ON EARTH...BUT, GOD HELP ME, **I LOVE IT.**"

ONE MINUTE 'TIL THE VOTE. LOOKS LIKE MOST FOLKS'VE MADE UP THEIR MINDS ALREADY, JOE.

APPEARANCES CAN BE DECEPTIVE, CHIEF JUDGE.

YEAH. SURE HOPE SO, ANYHOW.

HELL OF A RISK WE'RE TAKING HERE...

BUT A VITAL ONE.

THE DEMOCRATS HAVE GOT THE CITIZENS ON A KNIFE EDGE, HERSHEY. IT'S NOT ENOUGH TO JUST LAY IN WITH THE DAYSTICKS ANY MORE — THAT'S JUST STORING UP MORE TROUBLE.

NO, IF WE WANT TO CARRY ON WITH THE HEAVY DISCIPLINE THEN WE — AND THEY — HAVE TO KNOW THEY WANT IT.

THAT'S TRUE, JOE.

AND ANY SECOND NOW WE'RE GONNA KNOW ALRIGHT.

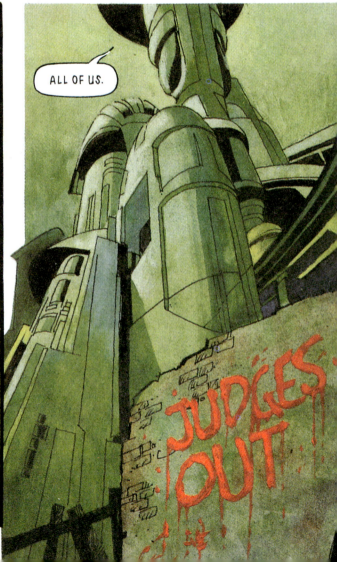

ALL OF US.

JUDGES OUT

NEXT PROG: SWEET LAND OF LIBERTY?

REFERENDUM DAY, MEGA-CITY ONE.

JUDGE DREDD

Twilight's Last Gleaming Part 2

Script **GARTH ENNIS**
Art **JOHN BURNS**
Lettering **TOM FRAME**

PERHAPS EVEN THE **CITY** HOLDS ITS BREATH AS ITS CHILDREN VOTE ON THEIR FUTURE.

A HUSH LIES OVER THE CONCRETE JUNGLE, A SILENCE SO KISSED WITH DESTINY THAT IT **SCREAMS** THROUGH THE PEDWAYS AND ZOOM TUBES, AROUND THE BLOCKS AND MEZZANINES TO ECHO ACROSS THIS VAST METROPOLIS ON THIS HISTORIC DAY.

CAN YOU HEAR IT...?

DREDD CAN.

NOON. THE CITIZENS VOTE.

THUS THE CITIZENS WILL HAVE TO WAIT QUITE A BIT LONGER THAN IF THE VOTES WERE BEING TABULATED BY CURRENT MEGA-CITY TECHNOLOGY... ABOUT SIX MINUTES.

THE VOTES UPLOAD DIRECTLY INTO THE BALLOTEER MAINFRAME COMPUTER, BUILT IN 2067 FOR THE LAST PRESIDENTIAL ELECTION AND DUSTED OFF ESPECIALLY FOR THE FIRST REFERENDUM IN 46 YEARS.

THE CHOICE IS CLEAR —

We the People

JUDICIAL CONTROL...

OR DEMOCRACY.

THE IRON FIST OF THE LAW AND THE CERTAINTY OF RETRIBUTION. HARSH LAWS THAT MANY COULDN'T EVEN UNDERSTAND. THE GUN AND THE DAYSTICK.

OR —

RULE BY AN ELECTED GOVERNMENT, WITH LAWMAKERS AND LAWKEEPERS SEPARATE, EACH BALANCING THE OTHER'S POWER.

SOMETHING MOST CITIZENS HAVE NEVER KNOWN.

INTERFACE CH. MAINFRAME

A B

ARE YOU ALRIGHT, BLONDEL? DREDD'S A FASCIST **SCUMBAG**! HE TURNED THE MARCH INTO A SLAUGHTER, REMEMBER? HE THREW YOU IN THE **CUBES**!

HE GOT ME **OUT**, TOO.

THIS ISN'T JUST **ANYONE** WE'RE TALKING ABOUT, JON. IT'S **JUDGE DREDD**. YOU SAW THE VID REPORTS AFTER NECROPOLIS...

THE SISTERS OF DEATH BURNT HIS **FACE** OFF, AND HE JUST GOT RIGHT UP AND CAME BACK AND SAVED THE CITY! CAN YOU IMAGINE THE SHEER **GUTS** THAT MUST HAVE TAKEN?

I JUST WONDER SOMETIMES... WHY ARE WE FIGHTING A MAN LIKE THAT?

JEEZ, BLONDEL, YOU'RE NOT THINKING STRAIGHT. IT'S ALL THE STRESS OF THE VOTE... SO HE'S A TOUGH GUY. SO **WHAT**?

YOU SAID IT YOURSELF -- THE JUDGES'LL DO **ANYTHING** TO HANG ON TO THEIR PRECIOUS POWER! THEY **LOVE** IT!

WHY? THEY DON'T GET PAID, THEY DON'T HAVE LIVES OF THEIR OWN -- WHAT'S IN IT FOR **THEM**?

WHAT DO THEY **GET** OUT OF IT?

BLONDEL! JON! **THIS IS IT**!

RESULTS ARE IN, GUYS!

WELL, HERE WE GO, SWEETHEART...

IN A FEW SECONDS, THE JUDGES WON'T MATTER ANYWAY.

THIS IS THE MOMENT, PEOPLE. THE VOTES ARE IN AND ARE BEING DOWNLOADED DIRECTLY TO YOU NOW WITH NO HUMAN INTERVENTION.

GREETINGS, CITIZENS. I, THE RETURNING {clik} BALLOTEER MAINFRAME, CERTIFY THESE TO BE THE ACCURATE RESULTS OF THE {clik} REFERENDUM.

ONLY THIRTY-FIVE PERCENT OF CITIZENS EXERCISED THEIR GRUD-GIVEN RIGHT TO VOTE... THE POOREST TURN-OUT IN {clik} SEVENTY-FOUR YEARS.

IF YOU DON'T VOTE FOR FOR YOUR CANDIDATES, HOW DO YOU EXPECT THEM TO WIN?

GRUD! TWO HUNDRED CHANNELS AND THEY'RE ALL SHOWING THE SAME THING!

OF THE FORTY-THREE MILLION VOTES CAST, TWENTY-THREE PERCENT VOTED BOTH OPTIONS {clik} AND THUS FORFEITED THEIR VOTES.

"BETTER THE DEVIL YOU KNOW."

UH-HUH.

NINE PERCENT VOTED FOR THE {clik} DEMOCRATS...

AND SIXTY-EIGHT PERCENT FOR THE JUDGES.

THE JUDGES ARE DULY RETURNED FOR ANOTHER TERM OF OFFICE.

WE'RE NOT OUT OF THE WOODS YET, CHIEF JUDGE. THE DEMS AREN'T GOING TO BELIEVE A RESULT LIKE THAT FOR A SECOND, EVEN WHEN IT'S STARING THEM IN THE FACE.

I'VE HAD ALL RIOT SQUADS STANDING BY SINCE DAWN.

GOOD THINKIN'.

YEAH... LISTEN TO THIS.

A SHOCK RESULT THERE! LET'S GO OVER LIVE TO DEMOCRATIC LEADER BLONDEL DUPRE —

THE JUDGES MUST BE CRAZY IF THEY THINK THEY CAN GET AWAY WITH A STUNT LIKE THIS!

IT'S A FIX!

CONTROL TO CHIEF JUDGE McGRUDER! PLEASE RESPOND!

YO.

CHIEF JUDGE -- IF DREDD'S STILL THERE WITH YOU, YOU'D BETTER PUT HIM ON...

WE GOT TROUBLE.

NEXT PROG: ONCE AND FOR ALL...

FIX! FIX!

GO TO HELL, YOU CHEATING SCUMBAGS!

YOU WON'T GIVE US DEMOCRACY, WE'LL COME AND TAKE IT!

THIS IS NO GOOD, JON! THEY'LL **MASSACRE** EVERYONE!

HUH? WE CAN'T GIVE UP NOW, BLONDEL! THEY'LL HAVE WON!

AT LEAST WE'LL BE **ALIVE!**

JUDGES OUT! JUDGES OUT!

GUESS WE GOT OUR ANSWER. MAY AS WELL—

NO.

FIX! FIX! FIX!

THERE'S A BETTER WAY, CHIEF JUDGE. IT'LL SAVE LIVES -- AND IT'LL KILL ANY LAST THOUGHTS OF DEMOCRACY TEN TIMES AS DEAD AS AN ASSAULT UNIT COULD.

HUH?

HOLD ON TO THIS FOR ME, HERSHEY. I'LL BE BACK FOR IT.

I STARTED ALL THIS...

I'M GOING TO FINISH IT.

WHAT THE HELL-?

IS HE **CRAZY?**

IT'S A TRICK! BOUND TO BE!

I DON'T THINK SO.

DUPRE.

DREDD.

TAKING A BIT OF A RISK COMING OUT HERE ALONE, AREN'T YOU? THERE'S TWO MILLION PEOPLE HERE.

THERE'S ENOUGH FIREPOWER BACK THERE TO WIPE OUT TEN TIMES THAT NUMBER -- BUT I DON'T NEED THAT TODAY.

YOU'RE GOING TO TURN ROUND AND GO HOME PEACEFULLY, EVERY LAST ONE OF YOU. AND I'LL TELL YOU WHY.

WE DIDN'T FIX ANYTHING, DUPRE. THE REFERENDUM WAS CARRIED OUT FAIR AND SQUARE AND THE PEOPLE VOTED FOR US BECAUSE THEY CAN RELY ON US -- BECAUSE THEY KNOW WHERE THEY STAND.

WE DIDN'T HAVE TO FIX IT.

DEMOCRACY'S NOT FOR THE PEOPLE -- NOT BECAUSE WE SAY SO, BUT BECAUSE THEY DON'T WANT IT.

YOU PEOPLE ARE DREAMERS. THAT'S OKAY IN ITS PLACE, BUT NOT WHEN YOU WANT TO RULE -- TO MAKE THE LAW IN THIS CITY.

BECAUSE HERE, I AM THE LAW.

BUT-

LET'S HEAR IT, DUPRE.

I...

YOU ARE THE LAW, JUDGE DREDD.

BLONDEL, ARE YOU **CRAZY?** WE —

OH FOR GRUD'S **SAKE, JON! LEAVE IT!**

BLONDEL DUPRE DIDN'T GO HOME THAT DAY. SHE WENT BACK TO THE DESERTED DEMOCRAT H.Q. AND SAT THERE UNTIL NIGHTFALL, THINKING ABOUT HER BROKEN HEART...

AND HER SHATTERED DREAMS.

BLONDEL?

JON...

YOU WEREN'T AT THE APARTMENT, HON. I WAS WORRIED.

I'M ALRIGHT. WHERE ARE ALL THE OTHERS?

THEY JUST WENT HOME, ALL OF THEM. I DON'T UNDERSTAND...

OH, JON, IT'S SIMPLE... DREDD'S **RIGHT.** WE'RE JUST USELESS DREAMERS. IT TAKES SOMEONE SPECIAL TO RULE **THIS** CITY. NOT US... WE'RE JUST LIKE EVERYONE ELSE, ALL THE PEOPLE WHO DIDN'T BOTHER TO VOTE, WHO DON'T WANT THE TROUBLE. WE JUST TOOK LONGER TO REALISE IT, THAT'S ALL.

ALL WE CAN DO IS MAKE THE BEST OF WHAT WE'VE GOT.

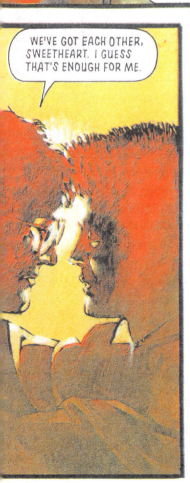

WE'VE GOT EACH OTHER, SWEETHEART. I GUESS THAT'S ENOUGH FOR ME.

HERE OR ANYWHERE ELSE.